First published 1990 by
Campbell Books
3/4 Bartholomew Place · London EC1A 7HH

ISBN 1 85292 065 3

Printed in Italy

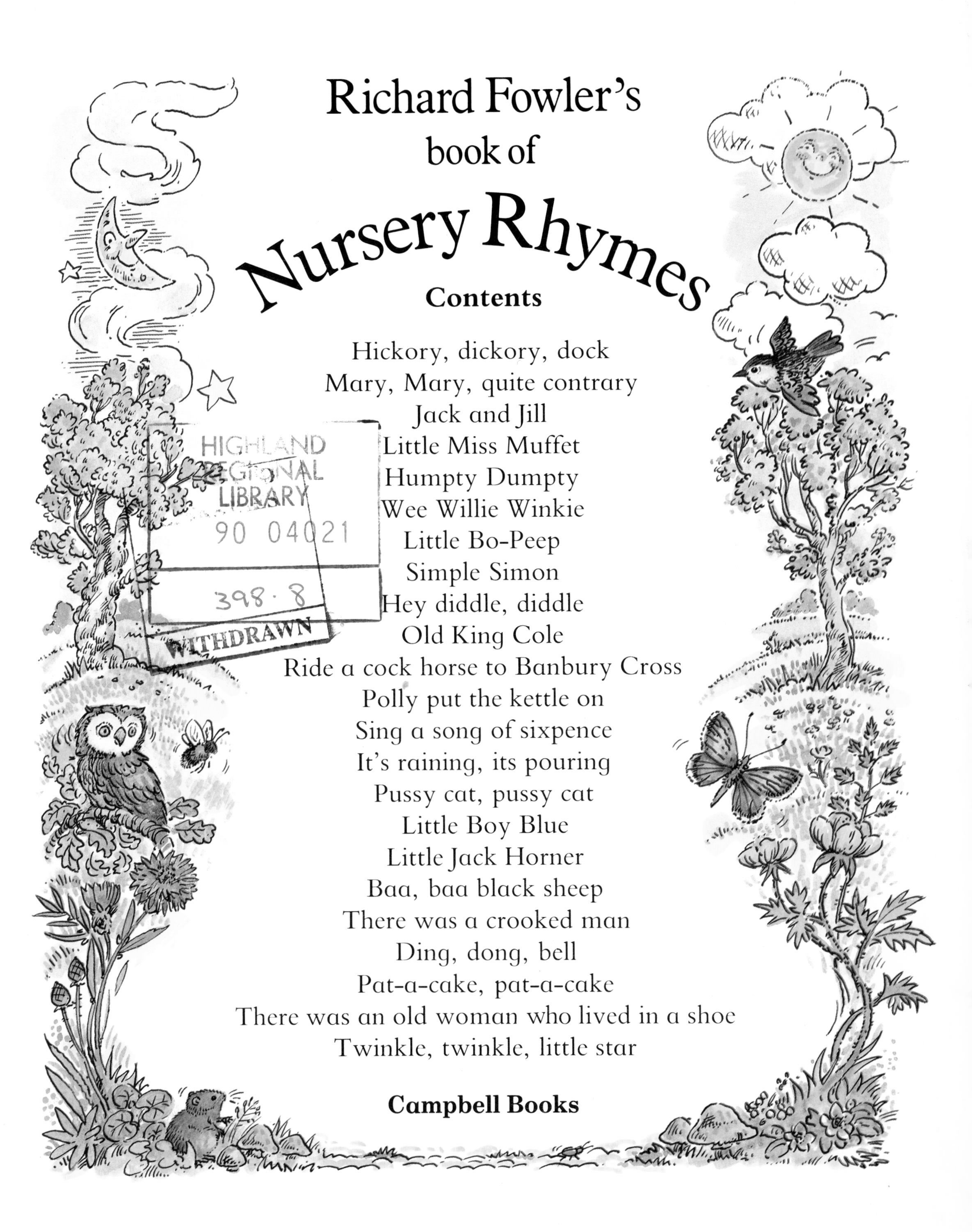

Richard Fowler's book of Nursery Rhymes

Contents

Hickory, dickory, dock
Mary, Mary, quite contrary
Jack and Jill
Little Miss Muffet
Humpty Dumpty
Wee Willie Winkie
Little Bo-Peep
Simple Simon
Hey diddle, diddle
Old King Cole
Ride a cock horse to Banbury Cross
Polly put the kettle on
Sing a song of sixpence
It's raining, its pouring
Pussy cat, pussy cat
Little Boy Blue
Little Jack Horner
Baa, baa black sheep
There was a crooked man
Ding, dong, bell
Pat-a-cake, pat-a-cake
There was an old woman who lived in a shoe
Twinkle, twinkle, little star

Campbell Books

Hickory, dickory, dock,
The mouse ran up the clock.
The clock struck one,
The mouse ran down,
Hickory, dickory dock.

Mary, Mary, quite contrary,
How does your garden grow?
With silver bells and cockle shells,
And pretty maids all in a row.

Jack and Jill went up the hill
To fetch a pail of water;
Jack fell down and broke his crown
And Jill came tumbling after.

Up Jack got and home did trot
As fast as he could caper;
Went to bed and bound his head
With vinegar and brown paper.

Little Miss Muffet,
Sat on a tuffet,
Eating her curds and whey.
Along came a spider,
Who sat down beside her,
And frightened Miss Muffet away.

Humpty Dumpty sat on a wall,
Humpty Dumpty had a great fall;
All the King's horses and all the King's men
Couldn't put Humpty together again.

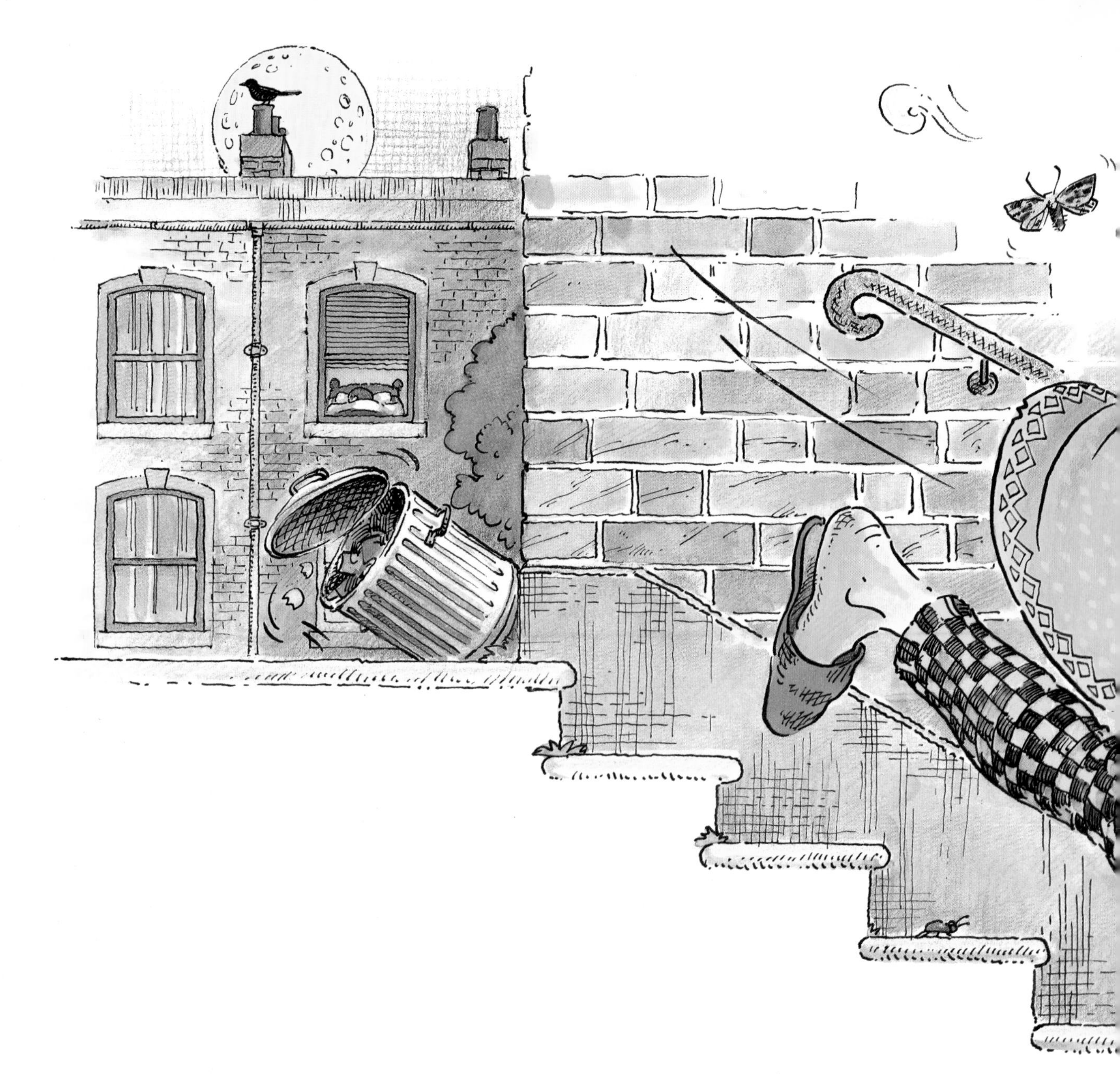

Wee Willie Winkie runs through the town,
Upstairs and downstairs in his nightgown,
Rapping at the window, crying through the lock,
Are the children all in bed, for now it's eight o'clock.

Little Bo-Peep has lost her sheep,
And doesn't know where to find them;
Leave them alone, and they'll come home,
Bringing their tails behind them.

Simple Simon met a pieman,
Going to the fair;
Says Simple Simon to the pieman,
Let me taste your ware.

Says the pieman to Simple Simon,
Show me first your penny;
Says Simple Simon to the pieman,
Indeed I have not any.

Hey diddle, diddle,
The cat and the fiddle,
The cow jumped over the moon;
The little dog laughed
To see such fun,
And the dish ran away with the spoon.

Old King Cole
Was a merry old soul,
And a merry old soul was he;
He called for his pipe,
And he called for his bowl,
And he called for his fiddlers three.

Every fiddler he had a fiddle,
And a very fine fiddle had he;
Oh, there's none so rare,
As can compare
With King Cole and his fiddlers three.

Ride a cock-horse to Banbury Cross,
To see a fine lady upon a white horse;
With rings on her fingers and bells on her toes,
She shall have music wherever she goes.

Polly put the kettle on,
Polly put the kettle on,
Polly put the kettle on,
We'll all have tea.

Sukey take it off again,
Sukey take it off again,
Sukey take it off again,
They've all gone away.

Sing a song of sixpence,
A pocket full of rye;
Four and twenty blackbirds
Baked in a pie.

When the pie was opened
The birds began to sing;
Wasn't that a dainty dish
To set before the king?

The king was in his counting house
Counting out his money;
The queen was in the parlour
Eating bread and honey.

The maid was in the garden
Hanging out the clothes;
Down came a blackbird,
And pecked off her nose.

It's raining, it's pouring,
The old man is snoring;
He went to bed and bumped his head,
And he couldn't get up in the morning.

Pussy cat, pussy cat, where have you been?
I've been up to London to see the Queen.
Pussy cat, pussy cat, what did you there?
I frightened a little mouse under a chair.

Little Boy Blue, come blow your horn,
The sheep's in the meadow, the cow's in the corn,
Where is the boy who looks after the sheep?
He's under a haycock fast asleep.
Will you wake him? No, not I,
For if you do, he's sure to cry.

Little Jack Horner
Sat in a corner,
Eating a Christmas pie;
He put in his thumb,
And pulled out a plum,
And said, "What a good boy am I!"

Baa, baa, black sheep,
Have you any wool?
Yes, sir, yes, sir
Three bags full;
One for the master,
And one for the dame,
And one for the little boy
Who lives down the lane.

BEST WOOL

BEST WOOL

There was a crooked man
And he walked a crooked mile,
He found a crooked sixpence
Against a crooked stile,
He bought a crooked cat,
Which caught a crooked mouse,
And they all lived together
In a little crooked house.

Ding, dong, bell,
Pussy's in the well.
Who put her in?
Little Johnny Green.
Who pulled her out?
Little Tommy Stout.
What a naughty boy was that
To try to drown poor pussy cat,
Who never did him any harm
And killed the mice in his father's barn.

Pat-a-cake, pat-a-cake, baker's man,
Bake me a cake as fast as you can.
Pat it and prick it, and mark it with B,
And put it in the oven for Baby and me.

There was an old woman who lived in a shoe,
She had so many children she didn't know what to do.
She gave them some broth without any bread;
She whipped them all soundly and put them to bed.

Twinkle, twinkle, little star,
How I wonder what you are!
Up above the world so high,
Like a diamond in the sky.